Daniel Chooses to Be Kind

P9-ELO-173

Adapted by Rachel Kalban
Based on the screenplay "King Daniel"
written by Becky Friedman and Angela C. Santomero
Poses and layouts by Jason Fruchter

Simon Spotlight

New York   London   Toronto   Sydney   New Delhi

SIMON SPOTLIGHT
An imprint of Simon & Schuster Children's Publishing Division
1230 Avenue of the Americas, New York, New York 10020
This Simon Spotlight paperback edition July 2017
© 2017 The Fred Rogers Company
All rights reserved, including the right of reproduction in whole or in part in any form.
SIMON SPOTLIGHT and colophon are registered trademarks of Simon & Schuster, Inc.
For information about special discounts for bulk purchases, please contact Simon & Schuster
Special Sales at 1-866-506-1949 or business@simonandschuster.com.
Manufactured in the United States of America 0617 LAK
10 9 8 7 6 5 4 3 2 1
ISBN 978-1-5344-0130-3 (pbk)
ISBN 978-1-5344-0131-0 (eBook)

It was a beautiful day in the neighborhood when Trolley drove up with King Friday. "I wonder what kings do all day?" Daniel said. "Maybe King Friday can tell us!"

"King Friday! King Friday! I have a question. What is it like being king?" asked Daniel.

"Hmmm . . . ," said King Friday. "If you really want to know . . . then I hereby declare you King Daniel for the day!"

"Really? Thank you!" said Daniel.

"King Daniel, you'll need to do everything left on this royal list," said King Friday. "First go to the bakery and pick up the most royally delicious treat. Next go to the music shop and get the loudest instrument. And last come to the castle with those two things."

"Grr-ific! Lets go!" said Daniel.

"Wait!" said King Friday. "I haven't told you the most important thing about being a king. You must be kind."

"What's kind?" asked Daniel.

"Being kind is doing a nice thing for someone, like helping them or giving them a hug. You can choose to be kind," explained King Friday.

"Okay!" answered Daniel. "I will be king and be kind. Let's go to the bakery!"

At the bakery Daniel and Mom saw that Baker Aker was very busy finishing his itsy-bitsy rolls.

Daniel remembered King Friday's words, "You can choose to be kind." He announced, "I can help you, Baker Aker!" and began working on the rolls.

"Thank you, Daniel," said Baker Aker.

"Remember to pick out a royally delicious treat, Daniel," said Mom.

"Right! Baker Aker, could we please have a banana muffin to bring to the castle?" asked Daniel. "It's my royal duty as king for the day."

"Good choice," said Baker Aker.

"Thanks! Have a royally grr-ific day!" said Daniel as they left the bakery.

Daniel and Mom were on their way when they saw O the Owl and his Uncle X.

"Royal greetings!" said Daniel.

"Hi, Daniel! I like your crown," said O. And just then his treat fell on the ground. "Oh no!" cried O. "That was my special treat!"

"O looks so sad. Maybe a new treat would help," said Daniel. "I think it would be kind to give O the banana muffin, don't you?"

"O, would you want this treat? It's a banana muffin," said Daniel.

"Really? You want to give it to me?" asked O. "Oh, thank you, thank you, thank you, Daniel. That is so kind of you!"

"You're welcome," said Daniel. "Being kind is tigertastic! I have to go to the music store now. Bye, O!"

"Good-bye, King Daniel!" O said.

Daniel and Mom went to the music shop. "Hi, Music Man Stan!" Daniel said.

"Well, hi there, Daniel," said Music Man Stan. Suddenly, a gust of wind blew away all his papers. "Oh no!" he exclaimed.

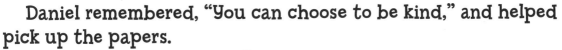

Daniel remembered, "You can choose to be kind," and helped pick up the papers.

"Thanks a bunch, Daniel," said Music Man Stan.

They went inside the music shop.

"Now, how can I help you?" asked Music Man Stan.

"I'm king for the day, and I am here to pick out the loudest instrument to take to the castle!" said Daniel.

"Well, pick out any one you would like," said Music Man Stan.

"I wonder which instrument makes the loudest sound," said Daniel.

He tried the triangle. *Ding!* It was not very loud.

He tried the maracas. *Shh, shh, shh, shake shake, shake.* They were not very loud either.

And next he tried the cymbals. *CRASH!* That was really loud! "I choose the cymbals," said Daniel.

"Now all I have to do is go to the castle. I don't have a royally delicious treat," said Daniel. "But at least I have a loud instrument for King Friday. Thank you, Music Man Stan!"

"You're welcome, King Daniel," said Music Man Stan.

On their way to the castle, Daniel and Mom Tiger saw Miss Elaina and Lady Elaine playing. Just then Miss Elaina dropped her doll in the mud. Miss Elaina began to cry.

"Oh no," said Daniel. "Miss Elaina is sad. I want to help her."

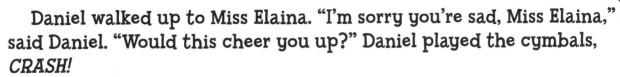

Daniel walked up to Miss Elaina. "I'm sorry you're sad, Miss Elaina," said Daniel. "Would this cheer you up?" Daniel played the cymbals, *CRASH!*

Miss Elaina smiled. "I love, love, love the cymbals! They are so loud! Can I have a turn?" she asked.

Miss Elaina banged the cymbals together. "This is the best!" she said.

Miss Elaina was so happy! Daniel wanted to give her the cymbals, but he was supposed to take them to the castle. Then Daniel remembered, "You can choose to be kind!"

"Miss Elaina, I declare that you can keep the cymbals," said Daniel.

"Oh thank you, thank you!" she said as she played happily.

"That was very kind, King Daniel," said Mom. "Now we better finish your royal duties."

"Okay," said Daniel. "Hear ye! Hear ye! King Daniel has to go to the castle now. Good-bye!"

As they arrived at the castle, King Friday announced, "Welcome, King Daniel! Did you bring everything I asked for?"

"No, King Friday," Daniel answered. "I don't have anything. I guess I didn't do a good job as king."

"Actually, Daniel," said King Friday, "being king is about helping others and being kind. I heard that you have found lots of ways to be kind today. I hereby declare that you have done your job as king very well!"

"Thank you, King Friday!" said Daniel.

"It was fun being king today. Did you know there are so many ways to be kind? Even the little ways make people so happy!" said Daniel. "Remember to be kind! Ugga Mugga!"